MARC BROWN

Try It, You'll Like It!

"Presenting my Lima Bean Luau Loaf," announced Dad.
"I'm practicing for the Elwood City Summer Luau next week."

"It smells funny," said D.W.

"Your father worked hard on this," said Mom. "Take a little taste..."

"Arthur was smart to go to Buster's for dinner," replied D.W. "I bet they're having hot dogs."

"You can have hot dogs any old day," said Dad. "Come on, D.W. Maybe you'll like it."

D.W. pushed her plate away.

The next day, Mom and Grandma Thora took D.W. with them for a hula lesson.

"I call this move the Waikiki Wiggle," said the hula teacher.

"This is fun!" said Grandma Thora.

"Come on, D.W., you can learn the hula with us," said Mom. "Give it a try."

"No," said D.W. "I'll look silly."

The morning of the luau, Arthur and D.W. went to pick up the leis.

"Try it on," said the florist.

"No thanks," said D.W.

"If you don't try new things," said Arthur, "you'll miss a lot of fun."

"I have plenty of fun," said D.W.

When they got home, Mom and Dad were busy getting things ready.

"I think Arthur and D.W. need to wear these," said Grandma Thora.

"I'm not wearing that," said D.W. "I'll look like a pineapple!"

"Yellow would be lovely on you," said Grandma Thora.

"No," said D.W. "I only wear pink or purple."

Arthur's friends were already at the park.

"Love your shirt, Francine," said Muffy. "Very fashionable."

"I like yours, too," said Francine. "Hey, great color, Buster."

ELWOOD CITY SUMMER LUAU

"Thanks," said Buster. "Wow, Arthur! Cool shirt."

"Where's your Hawaiian shirt, D.W.?" asked Francine.

D.W. looked down at her plain pink T-shirt. She didn't know what to say.

"Isn't that little girl too adorable?" said Muffy.

"Great shirt," said Francine.

D.W. went to find Grandma Thora.

"I think I'll try that shirt on now," said D.W.

"I brought it along just in case," Grandma said.

When D.W. looked at herself in the ladies' room mirror, she couldn't believe her eyes.

"I don't look like a pineapple," she exclaimed. "I look like a sunflower!"

"You look great!" said Francine. "Put this on and you're ready."

D.W. went to find Arthur.

"I still don't like yellow," she announced.

"You don't?" said Arthur.

"No!" said D.W. "I love it!"

Just then, a ukulele began to play.

"Arthur, watch me win the hula contest," said Francine.

"You need grace and beauty to do the hula," said Muffy. "That's why *I* will win."

"Try it, D.W." said Arthur.

"I don't think so," said D.W.

Suddenly D.W. felt something tickle her.

"The butterfly thinks I'm a sunflower," she said.

The butterfly liked her lei and flapped its wings against her neck.

"That tickles!" D.W. laughed.

It tickled so much, it made her wiggle.

D.W. wiggled and twirled.

"I thought she didn't want to dance," said Grandma Thora.

"I guess she changed her mind," said Mom.

"Look at D.W. go!" said Arthur.

"We have a hula contest winner," said the judge. "Would the young lady in the yellow Hawaiian shirt please come up and accept her prize?"

"Who me?" asked D.W.

"Cool dancing!" said Francine.

"What do you call that great step?" asked Muffy.

"I call it the 'Butterfly,'" D.W. said proudly.

After the hula contest, everyone lined up for the luau buffet.

"What is that?" asked Arthur.

"My pineapple mashed potatoes," said Dad. "Try some."

"No way!" said Arthur.

"I pass!" said Francine.

"Vomitrocious!" whispered Muffy.

D.W. took a big spoonful.

"These are delicious!" said D.W. "You guys should try them!"